The author would like to thank Dr Paul Thompson of the University of Aberdeen for his help and advice.

To Colette – J.B.

PUFFIN BOOKS

Published by the Penguin Group
Penguin Books Ltd, 27 Wrights Lane, London W8 5TZ, England
Penguin Books USA Inc., 375 Hudson Street, New York, New York 10014, USA
Penguin Books Australia Ltd, Ringwood, Victoria, Australia
Penguin Books Canada Ltd, 10 Alcorn Avenue, Toronto, Ontario, Canada M4V 3B2
Penguin Books (NZ) Ltd, 182–190 Wairau Road, Auckland 10, New Zealand

Penguin Books Ltd, Registered Offices: Harmondsworth, Middlesex, England

First published by Viking 1996
Published in Puffin Books 1997
1 3 5 7 9 10 8 6 4 2

Made and printed in Italy by Printers srl – Trento

THERESA RADCLIFFE

CIMRU THE SEAL

Illustrated by
JOHN BUTLER

PUFFIN BOOKS

The skies were dark and heavy over the bay. Cimru lay with her pup on the seaweed-covered rocks, waiting for the tide to lift them. The sea-birds flocked and whirled high above them, sensing the approaching storm.

The water rose at last, floating Cimru and her pup off the rocks. They bobbed together for a time on the gentle swell. Cimru kept her pup close, playfully nudging him in the small waves, watching over him. He would face many dangers in the coming weeks. Suddenly the storm broke. Black clouds thundered across the sky, whipping up the sea. The sea-birds flew inland, seeking shelter beyond the cliffs. But there was no shelter for Cimru and her pup.

The sea grew around them. Cimru swam with her pup, trying desperately to keep him beyond the breakers, but the wind and current swept him away, carrying him towards the shore. The waves took him, tumbling the little pup over and over in the treacherous foam, leaving him at last, bruised and weakened on the stony shore.

Out in the bay Cimru searched for her pup, diving again and again through the waves. Then, as the wind died down, she herself came ashore with the tide, not far from where the exhausted pup lay.

It was the great gull she saw first, huge wings beating, hovering as it prepared to swoop. Then she heard the cry. It was her pup's cry! A frightened whimper, a snarl. He was trying hopelessly to defend himself. Cimru lunged, snarling and furious, over the stones and the great gull wheeled away.

All that night Cimru lay with her pup, nursing him until his strength slowly returned.

The next day was warm and still. The sun shimmered high in the sky. The sea was blue and calm. Cimru and her pup swam back to the rocks. She was hungry herself now and needed food. She dived with him in the shallow water, catching what small fish and crabs she could. But there was not enough food here to satisfy her. She would have to hunt for fish in deeper water.

Leaving her pup asleep on the rocks, Cimru headed out for the open sea. She swam fast through the water, eagerly making for the spot where some gulls were swooping. Cimru soon caught one fish, then another, diving again and again, bringing only the largest of the fish to the surface.

Meanwhile, unknown to Cimru, some killer whales were moving fast around the next headland towards the bay. The whales were out hunting – hunting seals and their newly born pups. The largest whale, the male, swam ahead, his huge fin sweeping through the water. A female was calling her young calf to stay close.

Cimru heard the whales long before she saw them. For a second she froze. If they saw her now, so far from the rock, she would have no chance. She dived. She swam faster than she'd ever swum, using all her strength to reach the safety of the rocks. The whales arrived at the bay. They hung for a moment in the water, lifting their heads to look for prey. Cimru surfaced for air . . .

The whales tore through the water towards her, their dark fins cutting the waves. Closer and closer they came, diving as she dived, coming to the surface as she surfaced. They were moving in fast, forming a circle around her, trying to cut her off from the shore.

Cimru reached the rocks, just as the huge male swept past. As she hauled herself ashore, he lunged half out of the water towards her, jaws open wide. Cimru struggled towards her pup. The danger was not over yet. The tide was rising fast and before long the water would be over the rock. The whales were still there. They seemed to be waiting, circling the rocks, ready to take them.

Then at last the whales moved slowly away, perhaps to try their luck elsewhere. Only the diving sea-birds disturbed the quiet surface of the water. The danger had passed. For now Cimru and her pup were safe.